a minedition book
published by Penguin Young Readers Group

Text copyright © 2005 by Bruno Hächler
Illustration copyright © 2005 by Birte Müller
Original title: Was macht mein Teddybär die ganze Nacht?
Coproduction with Michael Neugebauer Publishing Ltd., Hong Kong.
Rights arranged with "minedition" Rights and Licensing AG, Zurich, Switzerland.
Published simultaneously in Canada.
Manufactured in Hong Kong by Wide World Ltd.
Typesetting in Veljovic book by Jovica Veljovic.
Color separation by Fotoreproduzioni Grafiche, Verona, Italy.

Library of Congress Cataloging-in-Publication Data available upon request.

ISBN 0-698-40029-1
10 9 8 7 6 5 4 3 2 1
First Impression

For more information please visit our website: www.minedition.com

*for my brother Sören,*
*from Birte*

Bruno Hächler

illustrated by

Birte Müller

translated by

Charise Myngher

# What Does My Teddy Bear Do All Night?

minedition

My teddy bear lies very still and waits for me at night.
I climb in bed and cuddle him and squeeze him really tight.
I love my little teddy bear.  He's soft, and cute, and sweet.
But when it's dark and time for bed, he doesn't want to sleep!

Goodnight teddy bear!

He tosses and he turns.
He rumbles and he rustles.
He reads a book,
and thinks big thoughts.
But he doesn't want to sleep!

Goodnight teddy bear!

Quietly he sneaks away and tiptoes
through the house.
I find his toys.  He's playing tricks.
But he doesn't want to sleep!

Goodnight teddy bear!

He whistles so I can find him.
Then he sings a silly song.
We stack my blocks and make a house.
But he doesn't want to sleep!

Goodnight teddy bear!

He needs to go, so I go too.
I wonder how late it is?
He tells a joke and makes me laugh.
But he doesn't want to sleep!

Goodnight teddy bear!

We jump up and down on my bed
until it starts to squeak.
I count to three, then he falls down.
But he doesn't want to sleep!

Goodnight teddy bear!

When Mom comes in to check on us
we lay there very still.
Teddy quickly turns out the light.
But he doesn't want to sleep!

Goodnight teddy bear!

Teddy bear, it's getting late.
The moon is shining bright.
My eyes are tired. Why aren't yours?
Why don't you want to sleep?

Goodnight teddy bear!

What is he planning next?
I know he's up to something...
I think I hear him fill up the tub.
But he doesn't want to sleep.

Goodnight teddy bear!

When shadows climb across my wall,
he won't let them get me.
My teddy bear stands up real tall
And watches over me.

My teddy bear doesn't leave my side.
He cuddles me all night.
I sleep all night and dream sweet dreams.
But he doesn't close his eyes.

When the bright sunshine wakes me up and the day
begins anew, I cuddle teddy in my arms
and smell his sweet perfume.
*Shhhhhhh...* I think he wants to sleep.

Suddenly I hear him snore.
He begins to sleep real deep.
I hug him tight.
He's worked all night.

...Now, I'll take care of you.
Goodnight teddy bear!